KING
HENRY VIII'S
SHOES

Roaring Good Reads will fire the imagination of all young readers – from short stories for children just starting to read on their own, to first chapter books and short novels for confident readers.

www.roaringgoodreads.co.uk

Some other Roaring Good Reads from Collins

Daisy May *by Jean Ure*

Elephant Child *by Mary Ellis*

Mister Skip *by Michael Morpurgo*

Spider McDrew *by Alan Durant*

The Witch's Tears *by Jenny Nimmo*

KING
HENRY VIII'S
SHOES

BY KAREN WALLACE

Illustrated by Chris Fisher

ROARING GOOD READS

Collins

First published in Great Britain by CollinsChildren'sBooks in 1995
This edition published by CollinsChildren'sBooks in 2003
Collins is an imprint of HarperCollins*Publishers* Ltd
77-85 Fulham Palace Road, Hammersmith, London W6 8JB

The HarperCollins website address is www.**fire**and**water**.com

1 3 5 7 9 8 6 4 2

Text copyright © Karen Wallace 1995
Illustrations by Chris Fisher 1995

ISBN 0 00 715843 2

The author asserts her moral right
to be identified as the author of the work.

Printed and bound in England by
Clays Ltd, St Ives plc

To Helen Lockwood,
who knows about shoes.

Chapter 1

Catherine Mortimer stared at the ceiling of the Great Watching Chamber at Hampton Court Palace. It looked like a gold and white jigsaw puzzle.

The room itself was enormous. Catherine imagined heavy oak tables stacked with roast boars' heads, stuffed geese and gigantic meat pies with pastry lids shaped to look like battle shields. She saw the light from hundreds of candles glittering in gold plates and goblets...

"Catherine Mortimer!" snapped Miss Stickler. "What did I just say?"

Miss Stickler was Catherine's history teacher. She was standing in the middle of Catherine's class on the other side of the chamber. She looked about as friendly as a striking cobra.

"Sorry," muttered Catherine. "I—" She looked up at the ceiling but Miss Stickler wasn't interested.

"You weren't listening," hissed Miss Stickler. "You never listen."

"I *do*," protested Catherine. Her face felt hot and red. She looked up at the ceiling again. "I was thinking—"

"And *I* was telling the class that Hampton Court Palace was the home of Henry the Eighth," interrupted Miss Stickler in a voice like a foghorn. "Henry the Eighth was one of England's finest kings." She glared at Catherine. "And what do *you* know about Henry the Eighth?"

The vision of the banqueting hall was still sharp in Catherine's imagination. She said the first thing that came into her head. "He ate a lot."

A noise somewhere between a cough and a snigger rippled through the rest of the class.

"*He ate a lot*," repeated Miss Stickler in such a way that Catherine knew she was in trouble.

Miss Stickler pressed her thin lips together. "On Monday morning you will present your project on King Henry the Eighth," she snarled. "Otherwise you stay behind on Monday afternoon."

"But the swimming competition is on Monday afternoon," cried Catherine. "And I'm in the team," she added miserably.

"Then I hope you will present a good project," said Miss Stickler in a mean voice. She turned to the rest of the class. "There's just time to visit the maze," she said. "We'll meet in the centre."

"This is a disaster," said a tall boy coming up to Catherine. His name was Edward Bailey and he was also in the swimming team. "What are you going to do?"

Panic began to creep across Catherine's

stomach like a puddle of cold water.

A plump red-haired girl called Anne Cartwright put her hand on Catherine's arm. "*No one* was listening. She just happened to pick on you."

Behind them was a loud *pop* and a strong smell of bubble gum.

"I can't *wait* for Monday morning," sneered a rubbery-faced girl called Stella Jakes. "History's my *favourite* subject."

She blew an orange bubble in Catherine's face. "And if you're worried about the competition, don't bother. Someone can always take your place."

"Like you, I suppose," said Catherine.

"Why not?" said Stella Jakes. She blew another bubble and swallowed it like a toad. "I'm just as good as you are."

"Then why weren't you chosen?" said Catherine angrily.

"Come on," said Anne, tugging at Catherine's arm. She jerked her head towards Miss Stickler's bad-tempered face glaring at them from the other end of the chamber. "If we don't hurry, we'll lose the others in the maze."

Catherine shook herself free. Angry tears welled up in her eyes. "You go," she muttered. Once again she looked up at the golden patterns in the ceiling. This time all the lines were blurred.

It was horribly unfair. How could Miss Stickler

possibly expect her to present her history project by Monday morning. It would mean working all weekend.

By the time Catherine had found the entrance to the maze, the others had disappeared inside. She could hear them laughing and calling over the high, thick hedges.

"Edward! Anne!" she shouted.

"Over here!" shouted Anne.

There was a snort of laughter. "Over *here*!" shouted another voice which sounded just like Stella Jakes.

Then there was the foghorn boom of Miss Stickler. "Time to go. Meet at the exit."

Catherine ran down one side of the maze trying to follow the sound of the voices. It was impossible. Every time she turned, she seemed

to get nearer the centre. Her heart began to
thump in her chest. If she was late for the
coach as well...

Suddenly the maze forked in front of her.
Catherine turned right. It was a dead end.

"Oh no!" she said out loud. Then, just as she was about to retrace her steps, something gold, half hidden in the roots of the hedge, caught her eye.

Even though she was going to be late, she *had* to see what it was. Catherine bent down and pulled the thing out.

It was a gold box – the strangest box she had ever seen. It was shaped like a duck's foot, wide at one end, narrow at the other and tied with a glossy purple ribbon. And it was embossed with a strangely familiar pattern.

Catherine stared at it. It was the same pattern as the one on the ceiling in Henry the Eighth's Great Watching Chamber. An odd feeling came over her. She had to keep this box because she knew there was something extraordinary inside it.

"Where's Catherine Mortimer?" roared Miss Stickler.

Quickly, Catherine unfastened her satchel and stuffed the gold box inside. Then, without making a single wrong turning, she ran straight to the exit.

It wasn't until she was sitting in the coach that Catherine began to wonder how on earth she had found her way out of the maze so easily.

Chapter 2

When Catherine went down to breakfast the next morning, there was a note from her mother on the kitchen table. 'Gone to Granny's. Make sure you eat some breakfast. Love Mum.'

Good, no one was at home. *Now* she could see what was in the gold box that she'd found yesterday in the maze.

She ran upstairs to her bedroom, unfastened her satchel and carefully lifted out the gold box. A faint smell of cloves filled the air.

It took ages to untie the purple ribbon because the knot was tight and her fingers felt like sausages. But Catherine was determined not to use scissors. It was bad luck to cut a ribbon.

At last she undid the final knot, then eased off the lid. The smell of cloves was stronger now. Inside there were layers of flimsy material as thin as gauze. With trembling hands, Catherine pulled them out.

At the bottom of the box was a parcel wrapped in stiff cream silk. It was narrow at one end and wide at the other.

Catherine could hear her heart banging in her ears. What would be inside it? A necklace? A dagger? An ancient map?

She unwrapped the stiff silk.

Inside was the most extraordinary shoe she had ever seen! It was made of purple velvet and, it too was shaped like a duck's foot.

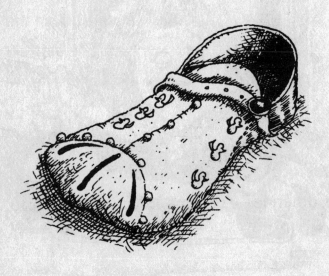

Tiny gold birds were embroidered along the sides and the seams were edged with pearls. Across the front, the strap was fastened by a turquoise stone.

Catherine turned the shoe upside down. The sole was made of leather and embossed in the same pattern as the gold and white ceiling at Hampton Court Palace.

There was a loud knock on the front door. "Catherine!" It was Edward's voice.

Catherine quickly put the shoe back in the box and stuffed it under her bed. She wanted to keep it her special secret just for a little longer.

She ran down to the kitchen and helped herself to a big bowl of cornflakes.

"Catherine!" This time it was Anne's voice.

"OK, I'm coming," shouted Catherine.

"Edward and I were worried about you," said Anne as they came into the kitchen. "You were so quiet on the coach going home yesterday."

"What's that funny smell?" said Edward.

Trump. Trump. Trump.

Heavy footsteps creaked across the ceiling.

"What's that noise?" said Anne. "I thought your dad worked on Saturdays."

"He does," said Catherine slowly. "And Mum's at Granny's."

The three children stared at each other.

Trump. Trump. Trump.

Catherine's face went white. "Someone's in my bedroom!" she whispered.

Creak. Creak. Creak.

"Someone's coming downstairs," said Edward. He edged over to where the kitchen knives were kept in a rack on the wall.

Creak. Creak. Creak.

The footsteps came down the stairs, along the front hall and stopped in front of the kitchen door. The smell of cloves was stronger than ever.

The children stood like statues, unable to move, barely able to breathe.

The kitchen door slowly opened.

Catherine heard Edward's knife clatter to the floor.

A huge man was standing in the doorway. He had a long face with a scraggy red beard which divided under his chin. His eyes were fierce and piggy. He was wearing a fur-trimmed doublet which billowed out under an embroidered jerkin. A gold medallion the size of a saucer hung from his neck.

Catherine, Edward and Anne stared with their mouths open.

The man standing in the doorway looked exactly like a portrait they had seen at

Hampton Court Palace – a portrait of King
Henry the Eighth!

Catherine's eyes moved from the huge man's face down his doublet to his white-stockinged legs. She gasped. He was wearing only one shoe! And it was just like the shoe she had found in the maze.

"I am King Henry the Eighth of England," roared the man. He glared at Catherine and pointed at his stockinged foot. "Fetch me my shoe!"

Catherine tried to say something but no words came.

"Zounds, child!" bellowed the king. "Will I have you beheaded? I said, fetch me my shoe!"

Chapter 3

Catherine ran upstairs to her bedroom. Her mind was whirling like a spinning top. On the one hand, she was fetching King Henry the Eighth's shoe. On the other hand, she knew that King Henry the Eighth had died over four hundred years ago, so whoever was standing in the kitchen must be a ghost.

But ghosts were supposed to be white, or at least see-through. This one was solid and in a steaming temper. He also looked very much alive.

Catherine grabbed the shoe and slid down the bannisters.

Anne was waiting for her outside the kitchen door. She stared at the shoe in Catherine's hand. "Where did you get *that*?" she cried, her eyes wide in amazement.

"I found it in the maze at Hampton Court," said Catherine. "Is he still there?"

Anne nodded. "If he's a ghost, he certainly isn't behaving like one," she said. "He wants me to roast your canary."

"What?"

Anne laughed. "He says he's hungry, and songbirds make good snacks."

"Well, he's not getting my canary," cried Catherine. She wasn't putting up with any nonsense from a loud-mouthed ghost, even if he was the King of England. She yanked open the kitchen door.

King Henry the Eighth had squashed

himself into a kitchen chair. There was a half-full measuring jug in his right hand and he was reading a mail order catalogue. He seemed to have forgotten all about his shoe and Catherine's canary.

Catherine stared at him. "What's in that jug," she whispered to Edward.

"My recipe for mead," said Edward proudly. "You know, that honey wine they drank in those days. I mixed honey and sherry and a chicken stock cube in your mum's blender."

"An excellent brew it is," bellowed the king, looking up from his catalogue. "What is your name, boy?"

"Edward, and this is Catherine, and this is Anne."

"I shall make you roasted cheese on toast, your Highness," said Anne, curtseying. "It's a special delicacy."

"And here is your shoe," said Catherine, bowing. There was no way Catherine was curtseying for anyone.

"Catherine, Anne and Edward," cried the king. "Why, those are my favourite names!" He took another swig from his measuring jug. "This calls for a celebration," he declared.

"What on earth is he talking about?" whispered Catherine to Edward.

"Henry the Eighth had six wives," muttered Edward. "Three Catherines, two Annes and a Jane."

Catherine's mouth dropped open. "And who was Edward?" she said. "His best man?"

"Edward was his son," explained Edward. "Didn't you learn *anything* yesterday? Look, why don't you ask him a few questions. You might get the project done, after all."

"That's a good idea," said Catherine slowly. In fact it was a completely crazy idea. How could you ask a ghost about a history project?

"Try it," said Edward grinning. "People love taking about themselves."

"But he's a ghost," said Catherine. "He might not like it."

As she spoke she stared at the huge man squashed into the tiny kitchen chair. He looked so real.

Edward laughed. "He can only have you beheaded!"

"Very funny," said Catherine, and she was

just about to speak when the king jumped up.

"I have come to a great decision," he cried. "You will know the French ambassador awaits me in my palace."

"Of course," said Edward smoothly.

"Excellent," said the king, looking pleased with himself. "Well, he shall wait a little longer. You children shall have the honour of my company."

He waved the mail order catalogue in the air. "Tell me, what wondrous things are these?"

Catherine crossed the room and looked over his shoulder at a double page of outsize ball gowns. She could see why he liked them. They had shiny beaded jackets and full satin skirts, but she didn't want to tell him they were women's clothes in case he was offended. "These are ball gowns, your Highness," she said.

Henry the Eighth's eyes glittered greedily. "And what is *this*?" He ran his finger under the words SHOPPING MADE EASY.

"Shopping is when people go and buy things they want," explained Anne.

The king gulped a mouthful of mead and banged his measuring jug on the table. "I *want* these things," he cried. "I *want* to go shopping!"

"What about the French ambassador?" asked Edward. "Will he wait that long?"

Henry the Eighth wrinkled his nose. "The French ambassador stinks of garlic and talks of war," he said. He glared at Edward. "And you sound like Cardinal Wolsey," he added in a sulky voice. "Always asking questions, always telling me what to do." He stamped his foot on the ground. "I am the king. Heads roll on my orders. The French ambassador will wait as long as I leave him. I *want* to go shopping."

The three children stared at each other.

"We could take him to Harrolds," said Catherine. "It's the biggest department store in town."

"Great!" said Anne. "I've never been shopping with a ghost – or a king, for that matter!"

"Especially one with a big mouth and old-fashioned ideas about execution," said Edward.

The king clapped his hands and wiggled his stockinged foot in the air. "Where are the servants in your palace," he demanded.

"We have no servants, your Highness," said Catherine.

"No servants?" cried the king. "I have one thousand servants at Hampton Court." He grabbed the shoe from Catherine's hand and jammed it on to his foot.

"Summon a chair," he ordered.

"Do you think he's expecting us to carry him?" whispered Catherine.

"My horse is lame," said the king, his voice rising. "The roads are muddy. Ruffians roam the countryside. SUMMON A CHAIR!"

"We travel by bus now, your Highness," said Anne. "It's faster and safer."

"And fit for a king," added Catherine quickly.

"Then SUMMON A BUS!" bawled King Henry the Eighth.

Chapter 4

"Now look here," said the bus conductor who was usually a patient man. "How can I charge your friend one fare when he is taking up two places?"

An empty bus had just happened to pull in to the bus stop and the king was convinced it had been summoned for him. Now he was refusing to share the front seat.

"This bus is mine," he shouted, waving an arm at the rest of the passengers who had boarded the bus. "These commoners shouldn't be here."

"Who are you calling common?" yelled an angry voice from the back.

"Wait for it," grinned Anne.

"Off with your head," bellowed Henry the Eighth.

"Off at the next stop," shouted the conductor grabbing the ticket out of Catherine's hand.

The bus stopped and they all climbed out. In front of them Harrolds was lit up with hundred of white lights. It looked like a fairy castle.

"Who does this castle belong to?" asked Henry the Eighth. "I want it."

"It's not a castle," explained Edward. "It's a department store."

"It's where people go shopping," said Anne.

"Excellent!" cried the king. "Then what are we doing standing out here?"

Edward rolled his eyes.

"Come on," said Catherine, pushing through the revolving door. "But we mustn't let him out of our sight."

She had forgotten that Henry the Eighth did not know about revolving doors.

The next minute the doors were whirling round and round, with the king stuck inside them.

"Oh, no!" cried Catherine, putting her hands over her face.

Edward went grey.

Anne collapsed in a heap, laughing.

"Disgraceful!" shrieked a voice. "A grown-up man behaving like a six-year-old!"

Catherine peeked through her fingers. A woman with a face like a granite cliff was waving an umbrella in the air.

"I have a train to catch!" she bellowed.

In front of her the doors were spinning by in a blur of glass. Inside, the king was making a noise like a bumblebee caught in a jam jar.

"I'm terribly sorry," muttered Catherine. "You see he's, um—" but she couldn't bring herself to say it. It sounded too crazy. "He's never been to a city before," she said. "He's from the country."

"Then he should stay there," snapped the woman who was wearing thick tweeds and heavy black boots with steel caps. "People like him belong in a farmyard." She jammed her foot under the spinning door.

The door stopped dead and Catherine watched in horror as Henry the Eighth flew through the air, landed on the far side of the crowded floor and disappeared.

"Oh no!" cried Catherine again. "We've lost him already!"

Edward shinned up a pillar, but he couldn't see the king anywhere.

"He's over there!" cried Anne. She dodged in and out of the jostling crowds with Catherine and Edward running behind her.

Suddenly they heard a great bellow of laughter. Far away in front of a cosmetic counter, Henry the Eighth was chatting to a shop assistant with long blonde hair and a wide red smile.

The shop assistant was holding a large bottle of perfume in her hand. It looked a bit like a bottle of wine.

"Hurry!" cried Catherine. "There's no time to lose!"

By the time the children reached the king, the shop assistant was handing him the bottle. "Would you like to try something different?" she asked batting her long black lashes.

"I certainly would!" said the king.

Catherine made a mad dash to come between them, but it was too late. The king poured the bottle of perfume down his throat.

"Filthy French poison!" he spluttered, tears running down his cheeks. He glared at the assistant with a face the colour of beetroot. "How dare you insult your monarch!" he bellowed.

The assistant glared back. Her wide red smile had frozen on her face. "Aren't you a bit old for fancy dress?" she asked coldly.

Anne grinned. "That's not fancy dress," she said proudly. "This is King Henry the Eighth of England."

"And *this* is the supervisor," said the shop assistant, pointing to a grim-faced man striding towards them.

There was a noise like a volcano rumbling. The king took a deep breath. His cheeks puffed out like a pair of bellows.

Catherine put her hands over her ears.

"Off with your head!" roared the king.

"Let's get out of here," cried Edward grabbing him by the arm.

"Where?" shouted Anne.

"Anywhere," cried Edward.

Ahead of them, Catherine saw a sign: 'BALL GOWNS – SUMMER SALE'. "Follow me!" she cried, and they rushed up the escalator pushing the king in front of them.

Chapter 5

Two hours later, Catherine, Anne and Edward watched as Henry the Eighth danced around a mountain of ball gowns.

"I want them all," he cried. "I *love* shopping!"

"But when will you wear them all?" asked Catherine. It was the sort of thing her mother might have said.

The king looked at her as if she was mad.

"Weddings and funerals, of course," he replied. He held up a swirling chiffon caftan and admired his reflection in a long mirror.

"You look lovely, your Highness," said Anne. "I particularly like the one with the blue satin hotpants."

"Do you, my sugar plum?" cried the king. "That is my favourite too." He patted Anne's knee with his pudgy hand. "Tell me," he said, "Do you think seven is a lucky number?"

"You mean, after three Catherines, two Annes and one Jane – another Anne?" said Anne with a grin on her face.

"Yes!" cried the king.

"No," said Anne firmly.

"My heart is a wounded dove tumbling from the sky," replied King Henry the Eighth, bending down on one knee.

"Is it really?" said Anne with her arms folded in front of her. "Well, you don't look that wounded to me."

The king struggled to his feet. "I can't understand it," he said in a sulky voice. "It's always worked before."

"All this shopping is making me hungry," said Edward, who hated shopping and mushy scenes at the best of times. "Let's go to BEEFCITY and get a hamburger."

"Songbird in a bun, your highness?" asked Catherine.

"An excellent idea," cried the king. He gave Anne a meaningful look. "The way to a man's heart is through his stomach," he told her in a serious voice. "I believe Catherine understands me better. Perhaps—"

"Come on," said Edward. He smiled at the sales lady who was slumped over the counter. "We'll take all the ball gowns, please," he said.

Henry the Eighth dropped a pouch of gold sovereigns on the counter. "And make it snappy," he added, beaming all over his fat face.

The sales lady heaved herself up. She had decided that this strangely-dressed man was a store detective in disguise and she was determined to get top marks for helpfulness even if he did pay in gold sovereigns.

Five minutes later, after Edward had convinced the king that it was *not* a good idea to change into the blue satin hotpants, they left the store with fifteen shopping bags and a free bottle of perfume. Henry the Eighth decided that it hadn't tasted so bad after all.

On the pavement the king declared that he liked cars and buses much better than horses. They were much faster and much louder. He held up his hand as a red bus sped towards them. "I'll summon a—"

"We'll walk," said Catherine quickly.

"Why walk when we could roar down the street making a terrible noise?" asked the king, looking disappointed.

"If we walk," said Catherine, thinking quickly, you can go *window* shopping.

The king brightened immediately. "What's that?" he asked.

"That's when you walk down a street and look in the shop windows," explained Edward. "Then if you see anything you want—"

"You have to write it down on a piece of paper," said Catherine in a solemn voice.

"But I don't have any paper," cried the king.

"I do!" said Anne. She pulled out a giant-sized notepad and a pencil from her bag.

"That won't be enough," said the king beginning to sound sulky. "I want *many* things."

"We can always buy another notepad," said Catherine.

Henry the Eighth *loved* window shopping. After ten minutes he wanted fifty television sets, a stuffed elephant, the whole window of a sweet shop and a caravan.

He was quite keen on a girl modelling bikinis but Anne said no. Buying other people wasn't allowed any more.

"But where are your stalls and marketplaces?" asked the king. "Where do people come to buy their fruit and vegetables?"

"Over there in the supermarket," said Catherine. She pointed to a big branch of *BINGERS* across the street.

King Henry the Eighth stared at the huge steel and glass building. "And where are the ovens to bake the people's bread?" he asked.

Again, Catherine pointed to the supermarket.

"And the butchers and the poultry-men and the fishmongers?" asked the king.

Once more, Catherine pointed to the supermarket.

The king looked long and hard through the plate glass windows at the brightly lit counters, the acres of food and the hundreds of servants filling trolleys for their masters.

"How do you spell *supermarket*?" he asked, licking the end of his pencil.

Chapter 6

BEEFCITY was a huge hamburger restaurant. It looked like a saloon bar in a cowboy town. The words BEEFCITY flashed from the nostrils of a five-metre high bull fixed on the roof. As soon as the king saw the bull, he added it to his shopping list.

Inside the restaurant, loud music played continuously. Coloured lights flashed on and off. And the whole place reeked of fried meat.

"A true banqueting hall," cried Henry the Eighth. "But why should our table be empty when everyone else's is full?" He lifted his ham-sized fist.

"This is a restaurant *not* a banqueting hall," said Catherine quickly. "Your food will come when you tell the waiter what you want."

"I want food," cried the king. "Is that not enough?"

"No," said Edward, "it isn't. This is a menu. You choose which hamburger you like best then you tell the waiter. Then he brings it to your table."

"What is a *hamburger*?" asked the king, narrowing his eyes.

Anne pointed to a monster hamburger on the next door table. "That is," she said.

"What?" cried the king. "But that is a mere mouthful. I want twenty of those."

The waiter couldn't believe his ears when he took their order. "Are you sure you can eat all of this?" he kept asking.

"Are you doubting the word of your king?" said Henry the Eighth in a low, dangerous voice.

"What about chips?" said Anne quickly.

"Chips of what?" asked Henry the Eighth.

"Potato chips, of course," said Anne.

The king looked puzzled.

"They didn't have potatoes then," said Edward. "It was bread and more bread."

"Quite right," said Henry the Eighth. "I want bread and more bread. I like bread."

He picked up a fork. "What's *this*," he asked.

"It's a fork," said Catherine. "You eat your food with it,"

"I don't," said Henry the Eighth. "A knife is all that's needed... and a trencher."

Now it was Catherine's turn to look puzzled. "What's a trencher?" she said.

"A wooden plate or a lump of bread," said Henry the Eighth. He smacked his lips. "Something to put your food on."

"It doesn't sound very *clean*," said Catherine.

"What does that matter if you are hungry," said the king. "A man wipes his knife on his breeches, that is enough."

Ten minutes later, three trolleys packed with hamburgers, fried onions, chips, two huge bottles of ketchup and four bowls of relish were dragged to the edge of their table.

"Enjoy your—" began the waiter. But he couldn't think of the right word and left them to it.

The king watched carefully as Edward, Catherine and Anne each lifted the top off their bun, poured some ketchup over the hamburger and then spread a little relish over it. It all looked a bit fiddly to him.

He arranged his twenty hamburgers in four rows of five, emptied an entire bottle of ketchup over the lot and upturned two bowls of relish on top of that.

Then he picked up his knife, speared a hamburger and shoved it in his mouth.

"Only peasants eat with their fingers," he told them, as ketchup ran down his chin and he sprayed bits of hamburger all over the table.

Catherine chewed her hamburger. Something about eating the same food as Henry the Eighth gave her the courage to ask the question that had been on her mind since she had first seen him in the door of her kitchen.

"How did you lose your shoe, your Highness?" she asked. "And how did I find it over four hundred years later?"

The king looked up and smiled. "I have absolutely no idea," he replied. "Something to do with the French ambassador, I'll warrant. Those French are always up to tricks. Mind you," he added, wiping his mouth on his sleeve, "I've been greatly entertained fetching it back, so perhaps I'll offer him peace terms, next time."

"Are you fighting a war?" asked Catherine.

"We're always fighting with the French," said Henry the Eighth, spearing another hamburger. "Or the Spanish. Or the Pope."

Catherine thought about the pattern that was embossed on the gold shoe box and the ceiling in the Great Watching Chamber at Hampton Court. She remembered the vision she had of the table covered in food, and the candlelight glittering in the gold plates.

"Do you ever have banquets in that big room with the gold ceiling at Hampton Court?" she asked.

The king's eyes lit up. "We certainly do," he said. "Last night we floated down the river in my barge disguised as shepherds in gold and red smocks. Cardinal Wolsey put on a banquet in the chamber. We had roast boar, stuffed geese and huge meat pies with pastry lids that looked like battle shields."

He slapped his thigh. Half a hamburger and a huge snort of laughter burst from his lips.

"On Monday night, I shall wear my blue satin hotpants," he cried. "The French ambassador will be so jealous. I shall look, how do you say it; s-e-n-s-a-t-i-o-n-a-l!" He rolled the word in his mouth like a great lump of chocolate.

On Monday morning, thought Catherine, I have to present my history project on Henry the Eighth. She stared at the huge man across the table. His gold medallion had an onion ring hanging off it, but his glassy blue eyes were watching her as if he was reading her mind.

Just then there was a loud *pop* behind them. Catherine stiffened. There was only one person who made a noise like that.

Stella Jakes leaned against their table and stared at Henry the Eighth. "Been to a pantomime then?" she asked Catherine. She swallowed her bubble of gum. "Some of us went to *swimming* practice."

"What are you talking about," said Edward. "You're not in the team."

"I am now," said Stella Jakes. "Sad thing is, Catherine's not."

"Then you lied to the coach," said Catherine. "You told him I wouldn't be there on Monday."

"Did I?" asked Stella Jakes. She turned and stared at Henry the Eighth. "Who's your fat friend?"

"Stella!" gasped Anne.

Henry the Eighth looked up and raised his eyebrows. "No friend of yours, Stella Jakes," he said in a quiet, menacing voice.

Stella Jakes opened her mouth to speak.
Then suddenly the colour drained from her
face and she ran from the restaurant as if she
had seen a ghost.

"What a pity," said Henry the Eighth.
"Stella Jakes seems to be sickening for
something." He smiled at Catherine.

"How do *you* know Stella Jakes?" gasped
Catherine."

"I *don't* know Stella Jakes," said Henry the Eighth, "but I recognize a weasel when I see one. And that weasel will not be troubling you again for a while." He gave her a look which said, don't ask questions, then he peered at the menu.

"How many knickerbocker glories shall I order?"

A huge weight floated off Catherine's shoulders. She didn't want to ask how or why, she just knew she wasn't worried about anything any more.

"Why not twenty?" she said with a grin. "One for each hamburger."

"Why not?" cried the king. "Then we must return. The French ambassador has waited long enough."

Chapter 7

On Monday morning, Catherine sat at her desk staring out of the classroom window. The glass was still dirty as always. The net still drooped on the tennis court outside.

In some ways nothing had changed. In other ways nothing would ever be the same again. Catherine looked up at the board. Miss Stickler had written CATHERINE MORTIMER – HENRY VIII on it.

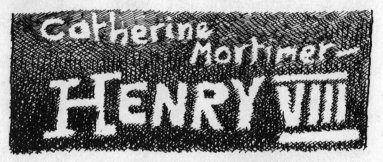

"Did we really take Henry the Eighth shopping?" whispered Anne, sitting down beside her. She looked flushed and excited as if she was holding on to a secret that kept trying to float away like a helium balloon.

"We did," said Catherine. "And we watched him eat twenty knickerbocker glories."

"And he sent Stella Jakes packing," said Edward. "What happened after we left?"

"We caught a bus home," said Catherine, "and he didn't make any fuss. When we got back to my house he told me to fetch the shoe box from my room. When I came down, he wasn't there."

"Did you tell your parents?" asked Anne.

"No," said Catherine with a grin. "Did you tell yours?"

Edward and Anne grinned back and shook their heads.

Anne looked around the class. "Stella Jakes isn't here," she said.

There was a *thwack* as a ruler hit the side of the blackboard.

"Places please," said Miss Stickler. "Catherine Mortimer will talk to us about King Henry the Eighth."

Edward and Anne watched as Catherine walked up to the front of the class and took out the giant notepad the king had used for a shopping list.

"I met Henry the Eighth this weekend," she said in a high clear voice. "He told me how he and his courtiers had dressed up as shepherds and how they travelled by barge down the Thames to a banquet at Hampton Court."

Miss Stickler's jaw dropped.

Edward winked at Anne and the two of them hid huge smiles behind their hands.

"He told me other things as well," said Catherine. And she went on to describe what the king wore, what he ate and what he had felt like, seeing things as they are today.

When Catherine had finished speaking, Miss Stickler got up from her chair. For the first time ever, she didn't look like a striking cobra. She looked overcome. She looked amazed.

"Catherine!" she cried. "That was *brilliant*!"

"Thank you," said Catherine. For one terrible moment she thought Miss Sticker was going to kiss her.

"I am so proud of you," cried Miss Stickler. "Your account was so vivid, so personal." She laughed. "It's almost as if you *had* met King Henry the Eighth at the weekend!"

"I did," said Catherine. But Miss Stickler didn't hear her because the other children in the class were cheering and stomping their feet.

"Quiet please," boomed Miss Stickler in her foghorn voice. "Now I have two announcements to make." As she spoke, a faint smell of cloves wafted into the air.

"Isn't that the smell—?" whispered Anne. Edward grinned and nodded.

"Catherine Mortimer has won a commendation for her history project on Henry the Eighth," said Miss Stickler. "And Stella Jakes has measles."

Catherine nearly fell out of her chair. She could have sworn she felt a heavy hand patting her on the shoulder!

Daisy May

Jean Ure

Illustrated by Karen Donnelly

For the first ten years of her life, Daisy lives in the Foundling Hospital with lots of other orphans. But on her tenth birthday she goes to work at the Dobell Academy for young ladies. There she watches, listens, learns and dreams. A 'rags-to-riches' story with a difference, where dreams really can come true!

ISBN 0 00 713369 3

An imprint of HarperCollinsPublishers

www.roaringgoodreads.co.uk